To:

....

From:

....

For Eunice — G.S.
For Grace — N.R.

First published in paperback in Great Britain by HarperCollins Children's Books in 2006

3 5 7 9 10 8 6 4 2

ISBN: 978-0-00-718006-6

HarperCollins Children's Books is a division of HarperCollins Publishers Ltd.

Text copyright © Gillian Shields 2006
Illustrations copyright © Nathan Reed 2006

The author and illustrator assert the moral right to be identified as the author and illustrator of the work.

Visit our website at: www.harpercollins.co.uk

Printed and bound in China

Angel Baby

Gillian Shields & Nathan Reed

HarperCollins *Children's Books*

Angel Baby is fast asleep,

dreaming of heaven and counting sheep.

Hungry Baby
wakes with a shout,
rattles his cot
and wants to get out.

Angry Baby roars himself red,

"Don't you know that...

...I WANT TO BE FED?"

Happy Baby visits his friends,

so many babies the fun never ends.

Thirsty Baby
sucks his bottle,
slurping and burping
and having a cuddle.

Busy Baby
loves to play
with bricks and blocks
and toys and clay.

Soapy Baby
loves his bath.
Daddy blows bubbles
to make him laugh.

Snuggly Baby
in Mummy's arms.
She sings a song,
that soothes and calms.

Tired Baby
has gone to bed
to rest his sweet,
little, sleepy head.

Shh...

...Angel Baby is fast asleep,

dreaming of heaven and counting sheep.